Henry Helps

Clean His Room

written by **Beth Bracken**   illustrated by **Ailie Busby**

PICTURE WINDOW BOOK
a capstone imprint

Henry Helps books are published by Picture Window Books
A Capstone Imprint
1710 Roe Crest Drive
North Mankato, Minnesota 56003
www.capstonepub.com

Library of Congress Cataloging-in-Publication Data

Bracken, Beth.

Henry helps clean his room / by Beth Bracken ; illustrated by Ailie Busby.

p. cm. -- (Henry helps)

Summary: Henry helps clean up his room.

ISBN 978-1-4048-7306-3 (library binding) -- ISBN 978-1-4048-7668-2 (pbk.) -- 978-1-4048-7917-1 (ebook)

1. Helping behavior--Juvenile fiction. 2. House cleaning--Juvenile fiction. 3. Orderliness--Juvenile fiction. [1. Helpfulness--Fiction. 2. Cleanliness--Fiction. 3. Orderliness--Fiction.] I. Busby, Ailie, ill. II. Title. III. Series: Bracken, Beth. Henry helps.

PZ7.B6989Hdc 2012

[E]--dc23

2011051242

Printed in the United States of America in North Mankato, Minnesota.
042012
006682CGF12

For Sam, the best helper I know. — BB

Henry has his own room!

He keeps his toys and books in his room.

He tries to put everything away
when he's finished playing,
but sometimes he forgets.

Then his room gets really messy.

"It's time to clean your room," Dad says.

"Okay," Henry says. "I'll help!"

The first thing Henry does is make his bed.

He puts his pillow at one end

and fixes his sheet.

Then Henry sets all of his books on his bookshelf.

He has a lot of books!

Trucks and trains and cars are next.

They go in colorful bins.

"Where should I put these stuffed animals?" Dad asks.

"They go on my bed," Henry tells him.

Dirty clothes go in the laundry basket.

Clean clothes go in the dresser.

Henry finds one of Toby's toys under his bed. That goes in Toby's mouth!

Now Henry's room is all clean!

"My room looks great!" he says.